# Mark
# Twain

---

## Tom Sawyer's
## Pirate Adventure

PENGUIN BOOKS

PENGUIN BOOKS

Published by the Penguin Group
Penguin Books Ltd, 27 Wrights Lane, London w8 5tz, England
Penguin Books USA Inc., 375 Hudson Street, New York, New York 10014, USA
Penguin Books Australia Ltd, Ringwood, Victoria, Australia
Penguin Books Canada Ltd, 10 Alcorn Avenue, Toronto, Ontario, Canada m4v 3b2
Penguin Books (nz) Ltd, 182–190 Wairau Road, Auckland 10, New Zealand

Penguin Books Ltd, Registered Offices: Harmondsworth, Middlesex, England

**First published in *The Adventures of Tom Sawyer* 1876**
**Published in Puffin Books 1950**

This extract published in Penguin Books 1996
1 3 5 7 9 10 8 6 4 2

Set in 12.5/13.5pt Bembo Monotype
Typeset by Datix International Limited, Bungay, Suffolk
Printed in England by Clays Ltd, St Ives plc

ONE of the reasons why Tom's mind had drifted away from its secret troubles was that it had found a new and weighty matter to interest itself about. Becky Thatcher had stopped coming to school. Tom had struggled with his pride a few days, and tried to 'whistle her down the wind', but failed. He began to find himself hanging around her father's house, nights, and feeling very miserable. She was sick. What if she should die! There was distraction in the thought. He no longer took an interest in war, nor even in piracy. The charm of life was gone, there was nothing but dreariness left. He put his hoop away, and his bat; there was no joy in them any more. His aunt was concerned; she began to try all manner of medicines on him. She was one of those people who are infatuated with patent medicines and all new-fangled methods of producing health or mending it. She was an inveterate experimenter in these things. When something fresh in this line came out she was in a fever right away to try it; not on herself, for she was never ailing; but on anybody else that came handy. She was a subscriber for all the 'Health' periodicals and phrenological frauds; and the solemn ignorance they were inflated with was breath to her nostrils. All the rot they contained about ventilation, and how to go to bed, and how to get up, and what to eat, and what to drink, and how much exercise to take, and what frame of mind to keep oneself in, and what sort of clothing to wear, was all gospel to her, and she never observed that her health journals of the current month customarily upset everything they had recommended the month before. She was as simple-hearted and honest as the day was long, and so she was an easy victim. She gathered together her quack periodicals and her quack medicines, and, thus armed with death, went about on her pale horse, metaphorically speaking, with 'hell following after'. But she never suspected that she was not an angel of healing and the balm of Gilead in disguise to the suffering neighbours.

2    The water treatment was new, now, and Tom's

low condition was a windfall to her. She had him out at daylight every morning, stood him up in the wood-shed and drowned him with a deluge of cold water; then she scrubbed him down with a towel like a file, and so brought him to; then she rolled him up in a wet sheet and put him away under blankets till she sweated his soul clean and 'the yellow stains of it came through his pores', as Tom said.

Yet notwithstanding all this the boy grew more and more melancholy and pale and dejected. She added hot baths, sitz baths, and plunges. The boy remained as dismal as a hearse. She began to assist the water with a slim oatmeal diet and blister plasters. She calculated his capacity as she would a jug's, and filled him up every day with quack cure-alls.

Tom had become indifferent to persecution by this time. This phase filled the old lady's heart with consternation. This indifference must be broken up at any cost. Now she heard of Painkiller for the first time. She ordered a lot at once. She tasted it and was filled with gratitude. It was simply fire in a liquid form. She dropped the water treatment and everything else, and pinned her faith to Pain-killer. She gave Tom a teaspoonful and watched with the deepest anxiety for the result. Her troubles were instantly at rest, her soul at peace again; for the 'indifference' was broken up. The boy could not have shown a wilder, heartier interest if she had built a fire under him.

Tom felt that it was time to wake up; this sort of life might be romantic enough in his blighted condition, but it was getting to have too little sentiment and too much distracting variety about it. So he thought over various plans for relief, and finally hit upon that of professing to be fond of Pain-killer. He asked for it so often that he became a nuisance, and his aunt ended by telling him to help himself and quit bothering her. If it had been Sid she would have had no misgivings to alloy her delight; but since it was Tom she watched the bottle clandestinely. She found that the medicine did really diminish, but it did not occur to her that the boy was mending the health of a crack in the sitting-room floor with it.

One day Tom was in the act of dosing the crack when his aunt's yellow cat came along, purring, eyeing the tea-spoon avariciously, and begging for a taste. Tom said:

'Don't ask for it unless you want it, Peter.'

But Peter signified that he did want it.

'You better make sure.'

Peter was sure.

'Now you've asked for it, and I'll give it to you, because there ain't anything mean about *me*; but if you find you don't like it you mustn't blame anybody but your own self.'

Peter was agreeable, so Tom pried his mouth open and poured down the Pain-killer. Peter sprang a couple of yards into the air, and then delivered a war-whoop and set off round and round the room, banging against furniture, up-setting flower-pots, and making general havoc. Next he rose on his hind feet and pranced around, in a frenzy of enjoyment, with his head over his shoulder and his voice proclaiming his unappeasable happiness. Then he went tearing around the house again, spreading chaos and de-struction in his path. Aunt Polly entered in time 5 to see him throw a few double summersets, deliver a final mighty hurrah, and sail through the open window, carrying the rest of the flower-pots with him. The old lady stood petrified with astonishment, peering over her glasses; Tom lay on the floor, expiring with laughter.

'Tom, what on earth ails that cat?'

'*I* don't know, Aunt,' gasped the boy.

'Why, I never seen anything like it. What *did* make him act so?'

''Deed I don't know, Aunt Polly; cats always act so when they're having a good time.'

'They do, do they?' There was something in the tone that made Tom apprehensive.

'Yes'm. That is, I believe they do.'

'You *do*?'

'Yes'm.'

The old lady was bending down, Tom watching with interest emphasized by anxiety. Too late he divined her 'drift'. The handle of the tell-tale teaspoon was visible under the bed-valance. Aunt Polly took it, held it up. Tom winced, and dropped his eyes. Aunt Polly 6 raised him by the usual handle – his ear – and cracked his head soundly with her thimble.

'Now, sir, what did you want to treat that poor dumb beast so for?'

'I done it out of pity for him – because he hadn't any aunt.'

'Hadn't any aunt! – you numskull. What has that got to do with it?'

'Heaps. Because if he'd a had one she'd a burnt him out herself! She'd a roasted his bowels out of him 'thout any more feeling than if he was a human!'

Aunt Polly felt a sudden pang of remorse. This was putting the thing in a new light; what was cruelty to a cat *might* be cruelty to a boy too. She began to soften: she felt sorry. Her eyes watered a little, and she put her hand on Tom's head and said gently:

'I was meaning for the best, Tom. And, Tom, it *did* do you good.'

Tom looked up in her face with just a perceptible twinkle peeping through his gravity:

'I know you was meaning for the best, Aunty, and so was I with Peter. It done *him* good, too. I never see him get around so nice –'

'Oh, go 'long with you, Tom, before you aggravate me again. And you try and see if you can't be a good boy for once, and you needn't take any more medicine.'

Tom reached school ahead of time. It was noticed that this strange thing had been occurring every day latterly. And now, as usual of late, he hung about the gate of the school-yard instead of playing with his comrades. He was sick, he said; and he looked it. He tried to seem to be looking everywhere but whither he was really looking – down the road. Presently Jeff Thatcher hove in sight, and Tom's face lighted; he gazed a moment, and then turned sorrowfully away. When Jeff Thatcher arrived, Tom accosted him, and 'led up' warily to opportunities for remark about Becky, but the giddy lad never could see the bait. Tom watched and watched, hoping whenever a frisking frock came in sight, and hating the owner of it as soon as he saw she was not the right one. At last frocks ceased to appear, and he dropped hopelessly into the dumps; he entered the empty school-house and sat down to 8 suffer. Then one more frock passed in at the gate, and Tom's heart gave a great bound. The next instant he was out, and 'going on' like an Indian; yelling, laughing, chasing boys, jumping over the fence at risk of life and limb, throwing handsprings, standing on his head – doing all the heroic things he could conceive of, and keeping a furtive eye out, all the while, to see if Becky Thatcher was noticing. But she seemed to be unconscious of it all; she never looked. Could it be possible that she was not aware that he was there? He carried his exploits to her immediate vicinity; came war-whooping around, snatched a boy's cap, hurled it to the roof of the schoolhouse, broke through a group of boys, tumbling them in every direction, and fell sprawling himself under Becky's nose, almost upsetting her – and she turned, with her nose in the air, and he heard her say, 'Mf! some people think they're mighty smart – always showing off!'

Tom's cheeks burned. He gathered himself up and sneaked off, crushed and crestfallen.

Tom's mind was made up now. He was gloomy and desperate. He was a forsaken, friendless boy, he said; nobody loved him; when they found out what they had driven him to, perhaps they would be sorry; he had tried to do right and get along, but they would not let him; since nothing would do them but to be rid of him, let it be so; and let them blame him for the consequences – why shouldn't they? what right had the friendless to complain? Yes, they had forced him to it at last: he would lead a life of crime. There was no choice. By this time he was far down Meadow Land, and the bell for school to 'take up' tinkled faintly upon his ear. He sobbed, now, to think he should never, never hear that old familiar sound any more – it was very hard, but it was forced on him; since he was driven out into the cold world, he must submit – but he forgave them. Then the sobs came thick and fast.

Just at this point he met his soul's sworn comrade, Joe Harper – hard-eyed, and with evidently a great and dismal purpose in his heart. Plainly here were 'two souls with but a single thought'. Tom, wiping his eyes with his sleeve, began to blubber out something about a resolution to escape from hard usage and lack of sympathy at home by roaming abroad into the great world, never to return; and ended by hoping that Joe would not forget him.

But it transpired that this was a request which Joe had just been going to make of Tom, and had come to hunt him up for that purpose. His mother had whipped him for drinking some cream which he had never tasted and knew nothing about; it was plain that she was tired of him and wished him to go; if she felt that way, there was nothing for him to do but to succumb; he hoped she would be happy, and never regret having driven her poor boy out into the unfeeling world to suffer and die.

As the two boys walked sorrowing along, they made a new compact to stand by each other and be brothers, and never separate till death relieved them of their troubles. Then they began to lay their plans. Joe was for being a hermit, and living on crusts in a remote cave, and dying, sometime, of cold, and want, and grief; but, after listening to Tom, he conceded that there were some conspicuous advantages about a life of crime, and so he consented to be a pirate.

Three miles below St Petersburg, at a point where the Mississippi river was a trifle over a mile wide, there was a long, narrow, wooded island, with a shallow bar at the head of it, and this offered well as a rendezvous. It was not inhabited; it lay far over towards the farther shore, abreast a dense and almost wholly unpeopled forest. So Jackson's Island was chosen. Who were to be the subjects of their piracies was a matter that did not occur to them. Then they hunted up Huckleberry Finn, and he joined them promptly, for all careers were one to him; he was indifferent. They presently separated, to meet at a lonely spot on the river bank two miles above the village, at the favourite hour, which was midnight. There was a small log raft there which they meant to capture. Each would bring hooks and lines, and such provisions as he could steal in the most dark and mysterious way – as became outlaws; and before the afternoon was done, they had all managed to enjoy the sweet glory of spreading the fact that pretty soon the town would 'hear something'. All who got this vague hint were cautioned to 'be mum and wait'.

About midnight Tom arrived with a boiled ham and a few trifles, and stopped in a dense undergrowth on a small bluff overlooking the meeting-place. It was starlight, and very still. The mighty river lay like an ocean at rest. Tom listened a moment, but no sound disturbed the quiet. Then he gave a low, distinct whistle. It was answered from under the bluff. Tom whistled twice more; these signals were answered in the same way. Then a guarded voice said:

'Who goes there?'

'Tom Sawyer, the Black Avenger of the Spanish Main. Name your names.'

'Huck Finn the Red-handed, and Joe Harper the Terror of the Seas.' Tom had furnished these titles from his favourite literature.

''Tis well. Give the countersign.'

Two hoarse whispers delivered the same awful word simultaneously to the brooding night:

'Blood!'

Then Tom tumbled his ham over the bluff and let himself down after it, tearing both skin and clothes to some extent in the effort. There was an easy, comfortable path along the shore under the bluff, but it lacked the advantages of difficulty and danger so valued by a pirate.

The Terror of the Seas had brought a side of bacon, and had about worn himself out with getting it there. Finn the Red-handed had stolen a skillet, and a quantity of half-cured leaf-tobacco, and had also brought a few corn-cobs to make pipes with. But none of the pirates smoked or 'chewed' but himself. The Black Avenger of the Spanish Main said it would never do to start without some fire. That was a wise thought; matches were hardly known there in that day. They saw a fire smouldering upon a great raft a hundred yards above, and they went stealthily thither and helped themselves to a chunk. They made an imposing adventure of it, saying 'hist' every now and then and suddenly halting with finger on lip; moving with hands on imaginary dagger-hilts; and giving orders in dismal whispers that if 'the foe' stirred to 'let him have it to the hilt', because 'dead men tell no tales'. They knew well enough that the raftmen were all down at the village laying in stores or having a spree, but still that was no excuse for their conducting this thing in an unpiratical way.

They shoved off presently, Tom in command, Huck at the left oar and Joe at the forward. Tom stood amidships, gloomy-browed and with folded arms, and gave his orders in a low, stern whisper.

'Luff, and bring her to the wind!'

'Aye, aye, sir!'

'Steady, steady-y-y-y!'

'Steady it is, sir!'

'Let her go off a point!'

'Point it is, sir!'

As the boys steadily and monotonously drove the raft towards mid-stream, it was no doubt understood that these orders were given only for 'style', and were not intended to mean anything in particular.

'What sail's she carrying?'

'Courses, tops'ls, and flying-jib, sir!'

'Send the r'yals up! Lay out aloft there, half a dozen of ye, foretopmast-stuns'l! Lively, now!'

'Aye, aye, sir!'

'Shake out that mainto-galans'l! Sheets and braces! *Now*, my hearties!'

'Aye, aye, sir!'

'Hellum-a-lee – hard a-port! Stand by to meet her when she comes! Port, port! *Now*, men! With a will! Stead-y-y!'

'Steady it is, sir!'

The raft drew beyond the middle of the river; the boys pointed her head right and then lay on their oars. The river was not high, so there was not more than a two or three mile current. Hardly a word was said during the next three-quarters of an hour. Now the raft was passing before the distant town. Two or three glimmering lights showed where it lay, peacefully sleeping, beyond the vague vast sweep of star-gemmed water, unconscious of the tremendous event that was happening. The Black Avenger stood still with folded arms, 'looking his last' upon the scene of his former joys and his later sufferings, and wishing 'she' could see him, now abroad on the wild sea, facing peril and death with dauntless heart, going to his doom with a grim smile on his lips. It was but a small strain on his imagination to remove Jackson's Island beyond eye-shot of the village, and so he 'looked his last' with a broken and satisfied heart. The other pirates were looking their last, too; and they all looked so long that they came near letting the current drift them out of the range of the island. But they discovered the danger in time, and made shift to avert it. About two o'clock in the morning the raft grounded on the bar two hundred yards above the head of the island, and they waded back and forth until they had landed their freight. Part of the little raft's belongings consisted of an old sail, and this they spread over a nook in the bushes for a tent to shelter their provisions; but they themselves would sleep in the open air in good weather, as became outlaws.

They built a fire against the side of a great log twenty or thirty steps within the sombre depths of the forest, and then cooked some bacon in the frying-pan for supper, and used up half of the corn 'pone' stock they had brought. It seemed glorious sport to be feasting in that wild free way in the virgin forest of an unexplored and uninhabited island, far from the haunts of men, and they said they would never return to civilization. The climbing fire lit up their faces and threw its ruddy glare upon the pillared tree-trunks of their forest temple, and upon the varnished foliage and festooning vines. When the last crisp slice of bacon was gone, and the last allowance of corn pone devoured, the boys stretched themselves out on the grass, filled with contentment. They could have found a cooler place, but they would not deny themselves such a romantic feature as the roasting camp-fire.

'*Ain't* it jolly?' said Joe.

'It's *nuts*,' said Tom.

'What would the boys say if they could see us?'

'Say? Well, they'd just die to be here – hey, Hucky?'

'I reckon so,' said Huckleberry; 'anyways *I'm* suited. I don't want nothing better'n this. I don't ever get enough to eat gen'ally – and here they can't come and kick at a feller and bullyrag him so.'

'It's just the life for me,' said Tom. 'You don't

have to get up, mornings, and you don't have to go to school, and wash, and all that blame foolishness.'

'You see a pirate don't have to do *anything*, Joe, when he's ashore, but a hermit *he* has to be praying considerable, and then he don't have any fun, any way, all by himself that way.'

'Oh yes, that's so,' said Joe, 'but I hadn't thought much about it, you know. I'd a good deal ruther be a pirate now that I've tried it.'

'You see,' said Tom, 'people don't go much on hermits, now-a-days, like they used to in old times, but a pirate's always respected. And a hermit's got to sleep on the hardest place he can find, and put sackcloth and ashes on his head, and stand out in the rain, and –'

'What does he put sackcloth and ashes on his head for?' inquired Huck.

'*I* dunno. But they've *got* to do it. Hermits always do. You'd have to do that if you was a hermit.'

'Dern'd if I would,' said Huck.

'Well, what would you do?'

'I dunno. But I wouldn't do that.'

19

'Why, Huck, you'd *have* to. How'd you get around it?'

'Why, I just wouldn't stand it. I'd run away.'

'Run away! Well, you *would* be a nice old slouch of a hermit. You'd be a disgrace.'

The Red-handed made no response, being better employed. He had finished gouging out a cob, and now he fitted a weed stem to it, loaded it with tobacco, and was pressing a coal to the charge and blowing a cloud of fragrant smoke; he was in the full bloom of luxurious contentment. The other pirates envied him this majestic vice, and secretly resolved to acquire it shortly. Presently Huck said:

'What do pirates have to do?'

Tom said:

'Oh, they have just a bully time – take ships, and burn them, and get the money and bury it in awful places in their island where there's ghosts and things to watch it, and kill everybody in the ships – make 'em walk a plank.'

'And they carry the women to the island,' said Joe; 'they don't kill the women.'

'No,' assented Tom, 'they don't kill the

women – they're too noble. And the women's always beautiful, too.'

'And don't they wear the bulliest clothes! Oh, no! All gold and silver and di'monds,' said Joe with enthusiasm.

'Who?' said Huck.

'Why, the pirates.'

Huck scanned his own clothing forlornly.

'I reckon I ain't dressed fitten for a pirate,' said he, with a regretful pathos in his voice; 'but I ain't got none but these.'

But the other boys told him the fine clothes would come fast enough after they should have begun their adventures. They made him understand that his poor rags would do to begin with, though it was customary for wealthy pirates to start with a proper wardrobe.

Gradually their talk died out and drowsiness began to steal upon the eyelids of the little waifs. The pipe dropped from the fingers of the Red-handed, and he slept the sleep of the conscience-free and the weary. The Terror of the Seas and the Black Avenger of the Spanish Main had more difficulty in getting to sleep. They said 21 their prayers inwardly, and lying down, since there was nobody there with authority to make them kneel and recite aloud; in truth they had a mind not to say them at all, but they were afraid to proceed to such lengths as that, lest they might call down a sudden and special thunderbolt from heaven. Then at once they reached and hovered upon the imminent verge of sleep – but an intruder came now that would not 'down'. It was conscience. They began to feel a vague fear that they had been doing wrong to run away; and next they thought of the stolen meat, and then the real torture came. They tried to argue it away by reminding conscience that they had purloined sweetmeats and apples scores of times; but conscience was not to be appeased by such thin plausibilities. It seemed to them, in the end, that there was no getting around the stubborn fact that taking sweetmeats was only 'hooking' while taking bacon and ham and such valuables was plain, simple stealing – and there was a command against that in the Bible. So they inwardly resolved that so long as they 22 remained in the business, their piracies should not again be sullied with the crime of stealing. Then conscience granted a truce, and these curiously inconsistent pirates fell peacefully to sleep.

When Tom awoke in the morning, he wondered where he was. He sat up and rubbed his eyes and looked around; then he comprehended. It was the cool grey dawn, and there was a delicious sense of repose and peace in the deep prevading calm and silence of the woods. Not a leaf stirred; not a sound obtruded upon great Nature's meditation. Beaded dewdrops stood upon the leaves and grasses. A white layer of ashes covered the fire, and a thin blue wreath of smoke rose straight into the air. Joe and Huck still slept. Now, far away in the woods, a bird called; another answered; presently the hammering of a woodpecker was heard. Gradually the cool dim grey of the morning whitened, and as gradually sounds multiplied and life manifested itself. The marvel of Nature shaking off sleep and going to work unfolded itself to the musing boy. A little green worm came crawling over a dewy leaf, 23 lifting two-thirds of his body into the air from time to time, 'sniffing around', then proceeding again, for he was measuring, Tom said; and when the worm approached him of his own accord, he sat as still as a stone, with his hopes rising and falling by turns as the creature still came towards him or seemed inclined to go elsewhere; and when at last it considered a painful moment with its curved body in the air and then came decisively down upon Tom's leg and began a journey over him, his whole heart was glad — for that meant that he was going to have a new suit of clothes — without the shadow of a doubt, a gaudy piratical uniform. Now a procession of ants appeared, from nowhere in particular, and went about their labours; one struggled manfully by with a dead spider five times as big as itself in its arms, and lugged it straight up a tree-trunk. A brown spotted lady-bug climbed the dizzy heights of a grass-blade, and Tom bent down close to it and said:

Lady-bug, lady-bug, fly away home,
Your house is on fire, your children's alone;

and she took wing and went off to see about it — which did not surprise the boy, for he knew of old that this insect was credulous about conflagrations, and he had practised upon its simplicity more than once. A tumble-bug came next, heaving sturdily at its ball, and Tom touched the creature, to see it shut its legs against its body and pretend to be dead. The birds were fairly rioting by this time. A cat-bird, the northern mocker, lit in a tree over Tom's head, and trilled out her imitations of her neighbours in a rapture of enjoyment; then a shrill jay swept down, a flash of blue flame, and stopped on a twig almost within the boy's reach, cocked his head to one side, and eyed the strangers with a consuming curiosity; a grey squirrel and a big fellow of the 'fox' kind came scurrying along, sitting up at intervals to inspect and chatter at the boys, for the wild things had probably never seen a human being before, and scarcely knew whether to be afraid or not. All Nature was wide awake and stirring now, long lances of sunlight pierced down through the dense foliage far and near, and a few butterflies came fluttering upon the scene.

Tom stirred up the other pirates and they all clattered away with a shout, and in a minute or two were stripped and chasing after and tumbling over each other in the shallow limpid water of the white sand-bar. They felt no longing for the little village sleeping in the distance beyond the majestic waste of water. A vagrant current or a slight rise in the river had carried off their raft, but this only gratified them, since its going was something like burning the bridge between them and civilization.

They came back to camp wonderfully refreshed, glad-hearted, and ravenous; and they soon had the camp-fire blazing up again. Huck found a spring of clear cold water close by, and the boys made cups of broad oak or hickory leaves, and felt that water, sweetened with such a wild-wood charm as that, would be a good enough substitute for coffee. While Joe was slicing bacon for breakfast, Tom and Huck asked him to hold on a minute; they stepped to a promising nook in the river bank and threw in their lines; almost immediately they had reward. Joe 26 had not had time to get impatient before they were back again with some handsome bass, a couple of sun-perch, and a small catfish — provision enough for a quite a family. They fried the fish with the bacon and were astonished; for no fish had ever seemed so delicious before. They did not know that the quicker a freshwater fish is on the fire after he is caught the better he is; and they reflected little upon what a sauce open-air sleeping, open-air exercise, bathing, and a large ingredient of hunger make, too.

They lay around in the shade after breakfast, while Huck had a smoke, and then went off through the woods on an exploring expedition. They tramped gaily along, over decaying logs, through tangled underbrush, among solemn monarchs of the forest, hung from their crowns to the ground with a drooping regalia of grapevines. Now and then they came upon snug nooks carpeted with grass and jewelled with flowers.

They found plenty of things to be delighted with, but nothing to be astonished at. They discovered that the island was about three miles long and a quarter of a mile wide, and that the shore it lay closest to was only separated from it by a narrow channel hardly two hundred yards wide. They took a swim about every hour, so it was close upon the middle of the afternoon when they got back to camp. They were too hungry to stop to fish, but they fared sumptuously upon cold ham, and then threw themselves down in the shade to talk. But the talk soon began to drag, and then died. The stillness, the solemnity, that brooded in the woods, and the sense of loneliness, began to tell upon the spirits of the boys. They fell to thinking. A sort of undefined longing crept upon them. This took dim shape presently – it was budding homesickness. Even Finn the Red-handed was dreaming of his door-steps and empty hogsheads. But they were all ashamed of their weakness, and none was brave enough to speak his thought.

For some time, now, the boys had been dully conscious of a peculiar sound in the distance, just as one sometimes is of the ticking of a clock which he takes no distinct note of. But now this mysterious sound became more pronounced, 28 and forced a recognition. The boys started, glanced at each other, and then each assumed a listening attitude. There was a long silence, profound and unbroken; then a deep, sullen boom came floating down out of the distance.

'What is it?' exclaimed Joe, under his breath.

'I wonder,' said Tom in a whisper.

'Tain't thunder,' said Huckleberry, in an awed tone, 'becuz thunder –'

'Hark!' said Tom; 'listen – don't talk.'

They waited a time that seemed an age, and then the same muffled boom troubled the solemn hush.

'Let's go and see.'

They sprang to their feet and hurried to the shore towards the town. They parted the bushes on the bank and peered out over the water. The little steam ferry-boat was about a mile below the village, drifting with the current. Her broad deck seemed crowded with people. There were a great many skiffs rowing about or floating with the stream in the neighbourhood of the ferry-boat, but the boys could not determine what the men in them were doing. Presently a great jet of white smoke burst from the ferry-boat's side, and as it expanded and rose in a lazy cloud, that same dull throb of sound was borne to the listeners again.

'I know now!' exclaimed Tom; 'somebody's drownded!'

'That's it,' said Huck; 'they done that last summer when Bill Turner got drownded; they shoot a cannon over the water, and that makes him come up to the top. Yes, and they take loaves of bread and put quicksilver in 'em and set 'em afloat, and wherever there's anybody that's drownded, they'll float right there and stop.'

'Yes, I've heard about that,' said Joe. 'I wonder what makes the bread do that.'

'Oh, it ain't the bread so much,' said Tom; 'I reckon it's mostly what they *say* over it before they start it out.'

'But they don't say anything over it,' said Huck. 'I've seen 'em, and they don't.'

'Well, that's funny,' said Tom. 'But maybe they say it to themselves. Of *course* they do. Anybody might know that.'

The others agreed that there was reason in what Tom said, because an ignorant lump of bread, uninstructed by an incantation, could not be expected to act very intelligently when sent upon an errand of such gravity.

'By jings, I wish I was over there now,' said Joe.

'I do too,' said Huck. 'I'd give heaps to know who it is.'

The boys still listened and watched. Presently a revealing thought flashed through Tom's mind, and he exclaimed:

'Boys, I know who's drownded; it's us!'

They felt like heroes in an instant. Here was a gorgeous triumph; they were missed; they were mourned; hearts were breaking on their account; tears were being shed; accusing memories of un-kindnesses to these poor lost lads were rising up, and unavailing regrets and remorse were being indulged; and, best of all, the departed were the talk of the whole town, and the envy of all the boys, as far as this dazzling notoriety was con-cerned. This was fine. It was worth while to be a pirate, after all.

As twilight drew on, the ferry-boat went back to her accustomed business and the skiffs disappeared. The pirates returned to camp. They were jubilant with vanity over their new grandeur and the illustrious trouble they were making. They caught fish, cooked supper, and ate it, and then fell to guessing at what the village was thinking and saying about them; and the pictures they drew of the public distress on their account were gratifying to look upon from their point of view. But when the shadows of night closed them in, they gradually ceased to talk, and sat gazing into the fire, with their minds evidently wandering elsewhere. The excitement was gone, now, and Tom and Joe could not keep back thoughts of certain persons at home who were not enjoying this fine frolic as much as they were. Misgivings came; they grew troubled and unhappy; a sigh or two escaped unawares. By-and-by Joe timidly ventured upon a roundabout 'feeler' as to how the others might look upon a return to civilization – not right now, but –

Tom withered him with derision. Huck, being uncommitted as yet, joined in with Tom, and the 32 waverer quickly 'explained', and was glad to get out of the scrape with as little taint of chicken-hearted homesickness clinging to his garments as he could. Mutiny was effectually laid to rest for the moment.

As the night deepened, Huck began to nod, and presently to snore; Joe followed next. Tom lay upon his elbow motionless for some time, watching the two intently. At last he got up cautiously on his knees, and went searching among the grass and the flickering reflections flung by the campfire. He picked up and inspected several large semi-cylinders of the thin white bark of a sycamore, and finally chose two which seemed to suit him. Then he knelt by the fire and painfully wrote something upon each of these with his 'red keel'; one he rolled up and put in his jacket-pocket, and the other he put in Joe's hat and removed it to a little distance from the owner. And he also put into the hat certain school-boy treasures of almost inestimable value, among them a lump of chalk, an indiarubber ball, three fish-hooks, and one of that kind of marbles known as a 'sure 'nough crystal'. Then he tip-toed his way cautiously among the trees till he felt that he was out of hearing, and straightway broke into a keen run in the direction of the sand-bar.

A few minutes later Tom was in the shoal water of the bar, wading towards the Illinois shore. Before the depth reached his middle he was half-way over: the current would permit no more wading now, so he struck out confidently to swim the remaining hundred yards. He swam quartering up stream, but still was swept downward rather faster than he had expected. However, he reached the shore finally, and drifted along till he found a low place and drew himself out. He put his hand on his jacket pocket, found his piece of bark safe, and then struck through the woods, following the shore with streaming garments. Shortly before ten o'clock he came out into an open place opposite the village, and saw the ferry-boat lying in the shadow of the trees and the high bank. Everything was quiet under the blinking stars. He crept down the bank, watching with all his eyes, slipped into the water, swam three or four strokes, and climbed into the skiff that did 'yawl' duty at the boat's stern. He laid himself down under the thwarts and waited, panting. Presently the cracked bell tapped, and a voice gave the order to 'cast off'. A minute or two later the skiff's head was standing high up against the boat's swell, and the voyage was begun. Tom felt happy in his success, for he knew it was the boat's last trip for the night. At the end of a long twelve or fifteen minutes the wheels stopped, and Tom slipped overboard and swam ashore in the dusk, landing fifty yards down stream, out of danger of possible stragglers. He flew along unfrequented alleys, and shortly found himself at his aunt's back fence. He climbed over, approached the 'ell' and looked in at the sitting-room window, for a light was burning there. There sat Aunt Polly, Sid, Mary, and Joe Harper's mother, grouped together, talking. They were by the bed, and the bed was between them and the door. Tom went to the door and began to softly lift the latch; then he pressed gently and the door yielded a crack; he continued pushing cautiously, and quaking every time it creaked, till he judged he might squeeze 35 through on his knees; and so he put his head through and began, warily.

'What makes the candle blow so?' said Aunt Polly. Tom hurried up. 'Why, that door's open, I believe. Why, of course it is. No end of strange things now. Go along and shut it, Sid.'

Tom disappeared under the bed just in time. He lay and 'breathed' himself for a time, and then crept to where he could almost touch his aunt's foot.

'But as I was saying,' said Aunt Polly, 'he warn't *bad*, so to say – only misch*ee*vous. Only just giddy, and harum-scarum, you know. He warn't any more responsible than a colt. *He* never meant any harm, and he was the best-hearted boy that ever was' – and she began to cry.

'It was just so with my Joe – always full of his devilment, and up to every kind of mischief, but he was just as unselfish and kind as he could be – and, laws bless me, to think I went and whipped him for taking that cream, never once recollecting that I throwed it out myself because it 36 was sour, and I never to see him again in this world, never, never, never, poor abused boy!' And Mrs Harper sobbed as if her heart would break.

'I hope Tom's better off where he is,' said Sid; 'but if he'd been better in some ways –'

'*Sid!*' Tom felt the glare of the old lady's eye, though he could not see it. 'Not a word against my Tom, now that he's gone! God'll take care of *him* – never you trouble *yourself*, sir. Oh, Mrs Harper, I don't know how to give him up, I don't know how to give him up! He was such a comfort to me, although he tormented my old heart out of me, 'most.'

'The Lord giveth, and the Lord taketh away. Blessed be the name of the Lord! But it's *so* hard – oh, it's so hard! Only last Saturday my Joe bursted a shooting-cracker right under my nose, and I knocked him sprawling. Little did I know then, how soon – oh, if it was to do over again I'd hug him and bless him for it.'

'Yes, yes, yes, I know just how you feel, Mrs Harper, I know just exactly how you feel. No longer ago than yesterday noon, my Tom took and filled the cat full of Pain-killer, and I did think the cretur would tear the house down.

And, God forgive me, I cracked Tom's head with my thimble, poor boy, poor dead boy. But he's out of all his troubles now. And the last words I ever heard him say was to reproach –'

But this memory was too much for the old lady, and she broke entirely down. Tom was snuffling now himself – and more in pity of himself than anybody else. He could hear Mary crying, and putting in a kindly word for him from time to time. He began to have a nobler opinion of himself than ever before. Still he was sufficiently touched by his aunt's grief to long to rush out from under the bed and overwhelm her with joy – and the theatrical gorgeousness of the thing appealed strongly to his nature, too, but he resisted and lay still. He went on listening, and gathered by odds and ends that it was conjectured at first that the boys had got drowned while taking a swim; then the small raft had been missed; next, certain boys said the missing lads had promised that the village should 'hear something' soon; and wise heads had 'put this and that together', and decided that the lads had gone off on that

raft, and would turn up at the next town below

presently; but towards noon the raft had been found, lodged against the Missouri shore some five or six miles below the village, and then hope perished; they must be drowned, else hunger would have driven them home by nightfall if not sooner. It was believed that the search for the bodies had been a fruitless effort merely because the drowning must have occurred in mid-channel, since the boys, being good swimmers, would otherwise have escaped to shore. This was Wednesday night. If the bodies continued missing until Sunday, all hope would be given over, and the funerals would be preached on that morning. Tom shuddered.

Mrs Harper gave a sobbing good night and turned to go. Then with a mutual impulse the two bereaved women flung themselves into each other's arms and had a good consoling cry, and then parted. Aunt Polly was tender far beyond her wont in her good night to Sid and Mary. Sid snuffled a bit, and Mary went off crying with all her heart.

Aunt Polly knelt down and prayed for Tom so touchingly, so appealingly, and with such measureless love in her words and her old trembling voice, that he was weltering in tears again long before she was through.

He had to keep still long after she went to bed, for she kept making broken-hearted ejaculations from time to time, tossing unrestfully, and turning over. But at last she was still, only moaning a little in her sleep. Now the boy stole out, rose gradually by the bedside, shaded the candle-light with his hand, and stood regarding her. His heart was full of pity for her. He took out his sycamore scroll and placed it by the candle. But something occurred to him, and he lingered considering. His face lighted with a happy solution of his thought; he put the bark hastily in his pocket, then he bent over and kissed the faded lips, and straightway made his stealthy exit, latching the door behind him.

He threaded his way back to the ferry landing, found nobody at large there, and walked boldly on board the boat, for he knew she was tenantless except that there was a watchman, who 40 always turned in and slept like a graven image.

He untied the skiff at the stern, slipped into it, and was soon rowing cautiously up stream. When he had pulled a mile above the village, he started quartering across, and bent himself stoutly to his work. He hit the landing on the other side neatly, for this was a familiar bit of work to him. He was moved to capture the skiff, arguing that it might be considered a ship and therefore legitimate prey for a pirate; but he knew a thorough search would be made for it, and that might end in revelations. So he stepped ashore and entered the wood. He sat down and took a long rest, torturing himself meantime to keep awake, and then started wearily down the home stretch. The night was far spent. It was broad daylight before he found himself fairly abreast the island bar. He rested again until the sun was well up and gilding the great river with its splendour, and then he plunged into the stream. A little later he paused, dripping, upon the threshold of the camp, and heard Joe say:

'No, Tom's true-blue, Huck, and he'll come back. He won't desert. He knows that would be a disgrace to a pirate, and Tom's too proud for 41 that sort of thing. He's up to something or other. Now, I wonder what?'

'Well, the things is ours anyway, ain't they?'

'Pretty near, but not yet, Huck. The writing says they are if he ain't back to breakfast.'

'Which he is!' exclaimed Tom, with fine dramatic effect, stepping grandly into camp.

A sumptuous breakfast of bacon and fish was shortly provided, and as the boys set to work upon it Tom recounted (and adorned) his adventures. They were a vain and boastful company of heroes when the tale was done. Then Tom hid himself away in a shady nook to sleep till noon, and the other pirates got ready to fish and explore.

After dinner all the gang turned out to hunt for turtle eggs on the bar. They went about poking sticks into the sand, and when they found a soft place they went down on their knees and dug with their hands. Sometimes they would take fifty or sixty eggs out of one hole. They were perfectly round, white things, a trifle smaller than an English walnut. They had a famous fried-egg feast that night, and another on Friday morning. After breakfast they went whooping and prancing out on the bar, and chased each other round and round, shedding clothes as they went, until they were naked, and then continued the frolic far away up the shoal water of the bar, against the stiff current, which latter tripped their legs from under them from time to time, and greatly increased the fun. And now and then they stood in a group and splashed water in each other's faces with their palms, gradually approaching each other with averted faces, to avoid the straggling sprays, and finally gripping and struggling till the best man ducked his neighbour, and then they all went under in a tangle of white legs and arms, and came up blowing, spluttering, laughing, and gasping for breath at one and the same time.

When they were well exhausted, they would run out and sprawl on the dry, hot sand, and lie there and cover themselves up with it, and by-and-by break for the water again and go through the original performance once more. Finally it occurred to them that their naked 43 skin represented flesh–coloured 'tights' very fairly; so they drew a ring in the sand and had a circus — with three clowns in it, for none would yield this proudest post to his neighbour.

Next they got their marbles, and played 'knucks' and 'ring-taw' and 'keeps', till that amusement grew stale. Then Joe and Huck had another swim, but Tom would not venture, because he found that in kicking off his trousers he had kicked his string of rattlesnake rattles off his ankle, and he wondered how he had escaped cramp so long without the protection of this mysterious charm. He did not venture again until he had found it, and by that time the other boys were tired and ready to rest. They gradually wandered apart, dropped into the 'dumps', and fell to gazing longingly across the wide river to where the village lay drowsing in the sun. Tom found himself writing '*Becky*' in the sand with his big toe; he scratched it out and was angry with himself for his weakness. But he wrote it again, nevertheless; he could not help it. He erased it once

more, and then took himself out of temptation

by driving the other boys together, and then joining them.

But Joe's spirits had gone down almost beyond resurrection. He was so homesick that he could hardly endure the misery of it. The tears lay very near the surface. Huck was melancholy too. Tom was downhearted, but tried hard not to show it. He had a secret which he was not ready to tell yet, but if this mutinous depression was not broken up soon, he would have to bring it out. He said with a great show of cheerfulness:

'I bet there's been pirates on this island before, boys. We'll explore it again. They've hid treasures here somewhere. How'd you feel to light on a rotten chest full of gold and silver – hey?'

But it roused only a faint enthusiasm, which faded out with no reply. Tom tried one or two other seductions; but they failed too. It was discouraging work. Joe sat poking up the sand with a stick, and looking very gloomy. Finally he said:

'Oh, boys, let's give it up. I want to go home. It's so lonesome.'

'Oh, no, Joe, you'll feel better by-and-by,' said Tom. 'Just think of the fishing that's here.'

'I don't care for the fishing. I want to go home.'

'But, Joe, there ain't such another swimming-place anywhere.'

'Swimming's no good; I don't seem to care for it, somehow, when there ain't anybody to say I shan't go in. I mean to go home.'

'Oh, shucks! baby! You want to see your mother, I reckon.'

'Yes, I *do* want to see my mother, and you would too, if you had one. I ain't any more baby than you are.' And Joe snuffled a little.

'Well, we'll let the cry-baby go home to his mother, won't we, Huck? Poor thing – does it want to see its mother? And so it shall. *You* like it here, don't you, Huck? We'll stay, won't we?'

Huck said 'Y-e-s –' without any heart in it.

'I'll never speak to you again as long as I live,' said Joe, rising. 'There now!' And he moved moodily away and began to dress himself.

'Who cares?' said Tom. 'Nobody wants you to. Go 'long home and get laughed at. Oh, you're a nice pirate. Huck and me ain't cry-babies. We'll stay, won't we, Huck? Let him go if he wants to. I reckon we can get along without him, per'aps.'

But Tom was uneasy nevertheless, and was alarmed to see Joe go sullenly on with his dressing. And then it was discomforting to see Huck eyeing Joe's preparations so wistfully, and keeping up such an ominous silence. Presently, without a parting word, Joe began to wade off towards the Illinois shore. Tom's heart began to sink. He glanced at Huck. Huck could not bear the look, and dropped his eyes. Then he said:

'I want to go too, Tom; it was getting so lonesome anyway, and now it'll be worse. Let's go too, Tom.'

'I won't; you can all go if you want to. I mean to stay.'

'Tom, I better go.'

'Well, go 'long – who's hindering you?'

Huck began to pick up his scattered clothes. He said:

'Tom, I wisht you'd come too. Now, you think it over. We'll wait for you when we get to shore.'

'Well, you'll wait a blame long time, that's all.'

Huck started sorrowfully away, and Tom

stood looking after him, with a strong desire tugging at his heart to yield his pride and go along too. He hoped the boys would stop, but they still waded slowly on. It suddenly dawned on Tom that it was become very lonely and still. He made one final struggle with his pride, and then he darted after his comrades, yelling:

'Wait! wait! I want to tell you something!'

They presently stopped and turned round. When he got to where they were, he began unfolding his secret, and they listened moodily till at last they saw the 'point' he was driving at, and then they set up a war-whoop of applause and said it was 'splendid!' and said if he had told them that at first, they wouldn't have started away. He made a plausible excuse; but his real reason had been the fear that not even the secret would keep them with him any very great length of time, and so he had meant to hold it in reserve as a last seduction.

The lads came gaily back and went at their sports again with a will, chatting all the time about Tom's stupendous plan and admiring the genius of it. After a dainty egg and fish dinner,

Tom said he wanted to learn to smoke now. Joe caught at the idea, and said he would like to try too. So Huck made pipes and filled them. These novices had never smoked anything before but cigars made of grape-vine, and they 'bit' the tongue, and were not considered manly, anyway.

Now they stretched themselves out on their elbows and began to puff charily, and with slender confidence. The smoke had an unpleasant taste, and they gagged a little, but Tom said:

'Why, it's just as easy! If I'd a knowed *this* was all, I'd a learnt long ago.'

'So would I,' said Joe. 'It's just nothing.'

'Why, many a time I've looked at people smoking and thought, Well, I wish I could do that; but I never thought I could,' said Tom. 'That's just the way with me, ain't it, Huck? You've heard me talk just that way, haven't you, Huck? I'll leave it to Huck if I haven't.'

'Yes, heaps of times,' said Huck.

'Well, I have too,' said Tom; 'oh, hundreds of times. Once down there by the slaughter-house. Don't you remember, Huck? Bob Tanner was there, and Johnny Miller, and Jeff Thatcher, when I said it. Don't you remember, Huck, 'bout me saying that?'

'Yes, that's so,' said Huck. 'That was the day after I lost a white alley – no, 'twas the day before!'

'There, I told you so,' said Tom. 'Huck recollects it.'

'I believe I could smoke this pipe all day,' said Joe. '*I* don't feel sick.'

'Neither do I,' said Tom. '*I* could smoke it all day, but I bet you Jeff Thatcher couldn't.'

'Jeff Thatcher! Why, he'd keel over just with two draws. Just let him try it once; *he'd* see!'

'I bet he would, and Johnny Miller – I wish I could see Johnny Miller tackle it once.'

'Oh, don't *I?*' said Joe. 'Why, I bet you Johnny Miller couldn't any more do this than nothing. Just one little snifter would fetch *him*.'

''Deed it would, Joe. Say – I wish the boys could see us now.'

'So do I!'

'Say, boys, don't say anything about it, and some time when they're around I'll come up to

you and say, "Joe, got a pipe? I want a smoke!"
And you'll say, kind of careless like, as if it warn't
anything, you'll say, "Yes. I got my *old* pipe, and
another one, but my tobacker ain't very good."
And I'll say, "Oh, that's all right, if it's *strong*
enough." And then you'll out with the pipes,
and we'll light up just as ca'm, and then just see
'em look!'

'By jings, that'll be gay, Tom; I wish it was
*now*!'

'So do I! And when we tell 'em we learned
when we was off pirating, won't they wish they'd
been along!'

'Oh, I reckon not! I'll just *bet* they will!'

So the talk ran on; but presently it began to
flag a trifle, and grow disjointed. The silences
widened; the expectoration marvellously increased. Every pore inside the boys' cheeks
became a spouting fountain; they could scarcely
bale out the cellars under their tongues fast
enough to prevent an inundation; little overflow-
ings down their throats occurred in spite of all
they could do, and sudden retchings followed
every time. Both boys were looking very pale 51

and miserable now. Joe's pipe dropped from his nerveless fingers. Tom's followed. Both fountains were going furiously, and both pumps baling with might and main. Joe said feebly:

'I've lost my knife. I reckon I better go and find it.'

Tom said, with quivering lips and halting utterance:

'I'll help you. You go over that way, and I'll hunt around by the spring. No, you needn't come, Huck – we can find it.'

So Huck sat down again, and waited an hour. Then he found it lonesome, and went to find his comrades. They were wide apart in the woods, both very pale, both fast asleep. But something informed him that if they had had any trouble they had got rid of it.

They were not talkative at supper that night; they had a humble look; and when Huck prepared his pipe after the meal, and was going to prepare theirs, they said no, they were not feeling very well – something they ate at dinner had disagreed with them.

★

About midnight Joe awoke, and called the boys. There was a brooding oppressiveness in the air that seemed to bode something. The boys huddled themselves together, and sought the friendly companionship of the fire, though the dull dead heat of the breathless atmosphere was stifling. They sat still, intent and waiting. Beyond the light of the fire, everything was swallowed up in the blackness of darkness. Presently there came a quivering glow that vaguely revealed the foliage for a moment and then vanished. By-and-by another came, a little stronger. Then another. Then a faint moan came sighing through the branches of the forest, and the boys felt a fleeting breath upon their cheeks, and shuddered with the fancy that the Spirit of the Night had gone by. There was a pause. Now a weird flash turned night into day, and showed every little grass-blade separate and distinct, that grew about their feet. And it showed three white startled faces, too. A deep peal of thunder went rolling and tumbling down the heavens, and lost itself in sullen rumblings in the distance. A sweep of chilly air passed by, rustling all the leaves and snowing the flaky ashes 53 broadcast about the fire. Another fierce glare lit up the forest, and an instant crash followed that seemed to rend the tree-tops right over the boys' heads. They clung together in terror, in the quick gloom that followed. A few big rain-drops fell pattering upon the leaves.

'Quick, boys, go for the tent!' exclaimed Tom.

They sprang away, stumbling over roots and among vines in the dark, no two plunging in the same direction. A furious blast roared through the trees, making everything sing as it went. One blinding flash after another came, and peal on peal of deafening thunder. And now a drenching rain poured down, and the rising hurricane drove it in sheets along the ground. The boys cried out to each other, but the roaring wind and the booming thunder-blasts drowned their voices utterly. However, one by one they straggled in at last, and took shelter under the tent, cold, scared, and streaming with water; but to have company in misery seemed something to be grateful for. They could not talk, the old sail flapped so furiously, even if the other noises would have allowed them. The tempest rose higher and higher, and presently the sail tore loose from its fastenings, and went winging away on the blast. The boys seized each other's hands, and fled, with many tumblings and bruises, to the shelter of a great oak that stood upon the river bank. Now the battle was at its highest. Under the ceaseless conflagrations of lightnings that flamed in the skies, everything below stood out in clean-cut and shadowless distinctness; the bending trees, the billowy river white with foam, the driving spray of spume-flakes, the dim outlines of the high bluffs on the other side, glimpsed throught the drifting cloud-rack and the slanting veil of rain. Every little while some giant tree yielded the fight and fell crashing through the younger growth; and the unflagging thunder-peals came now in ear-splitting explosive bursts, keen and sharp, and unspeakably appalling. The storm culminated in one matchless effort that seemed likely to tear the island to pieces, burn it up, drown it to the tree-tops, blow it away and deafen every creature in it, all at one and the same moment. It was a wild night for homeless young heads to be out in.

But at last the battle was done, and the forces retired, with weaker and weaker threatenings and grumblings, and peace resumed her sway. The boys went back to camp a good deal awed; but they found there was still something to be thankful for, because the great sycamore, the shelter of their beds, was a ruin, now, blasted by the lightnings, and they were not under it when the catastrophe happened.

Everything in camp was drenched, the camp-fire as well; for they were but heedless lads, like their generation, and had made no provision against rain. Here was matter for dismay, for they were soaked through and chilled. They were eloquent in their distress: but they presently discovered that the fire had eaten so far up under the great log it had been built against (where it curved upward and separated itself from the ground), that a hand-breath or so of it had escaped wetting; so they patiently wrought until, with shreds and bark gathered from under sides of sheltered logs, they coaxed the fire to burn again. Then they piled on great dead boughs till they had a roaring furnace and were glad-hearted once more. They dried their boiled ham and had a feast, and after that they sat by the fire and expanded and glorified their midnight adventure until morning, for there was not a dry spot to sleep on anywhere around.

As the sun began to steal in upon the boys, drowsiness came over them and they went out on the sand-bar and lay down to sleep. They got scorched out by-and-by, and drearily set about getting breakfast. After the meal they felt rusty, and stiff-jointed, and a little homesick once more. Tom saw the signs, and fell to cheering up the pirates as well as he could. But they cared nothing for marbles, or circus, or swimming, or anything. He reminded them of the imposing secret, and raised a ray of cheer. While it lasted he got them interested in a new device. This was to knock off being pirates for a while, and be Indians for a change. They were attracted by this idea; so it was not long before they were stripped, and striped from head to heel with black mud, like so many zebras, all of them chiefs, of course, and then they went tearing through the woods to attack an English settlement.

By-and-by they separated into three hostile tribes, and darted upon each other from ambush with dreadful war-whoops, and killed and scalped each other by thousands. It was a gory day. Consequently it was a satisfactory one.

They assembled in camp towards supper-time, hungry and happy. But now a difficulty arose – hostile Indians could not break the bread of hospitality together without first making peace, and this was a simple impossibility without smoking a pipe of peace. There was no other process that ever they had heard of. Two of the savages almost wished they had remained pirates. However, there was no other way, so with such show of cheerfulness as they could muster they called for the pipe and took their whiff, as it passed, in due form.

And behold they were glad they had gone into savagery, for they had gained something; they found that they could now smoke a little without having to go and hunt for a lost knife; they did not get sick enough to be seriously uncomfortable. They were not likely to fool away this high promise for lack of effort. No, they practised cautiously after supper with right fair success, and so they spent a jubilant evening. They were prouder and happier in their new acquirement than they would have been in the scalping and skinning of the Six Nations. We will leave them to smoke and chatter and brag, since we have no further use for them at present.

*Some Puffin books by Mark Twain*

THE ADVENTURES OF HUCKLEBERRY FINN
THE ADVENTURES OF TOM SAWYER
THE PRINCE AND THE PAUPER